GOOD-BYE, ARNOLD!

story and pictures by P. K. ROCHE

The Dial Press · New York

GOOD-BYE, ARNOLD!
is published in a hardcover edition by The Dial Press,
1 Dag Hammarskjold Plaza, New York, New York 10017.
ISBN: 0-8037-3033-0

The art for this book was prepared in black line drawings
with separations for red, yellow, and black wash.

With very special thanks to Uri Shulevitz,
who assured me that anyone could learn to draw.

For
Keith

Webster was lying in bed. He was thinking about why he hated his big brother, Arnold. There were so many reasons.

Arnold didn't share. He never let Webster have a turn sleeping in the top bunk. And he had toys and games that Webster was not allowed to put a paw on. Arnold was bossy and said he wasn't. And he even snored in his sleep and said he didn't. Worst of all, he was always around, acting important. Webster fell asleep before he could think of anything good about Arnold.

That night Webster had a dream that Arnold was leaving home.

.

The very next morning there was a phone call from Grandma. She invited Arnold to come and visit for a whole week.

"Whoopee!" said Arnold.

"I'll help you pack," said Webster.

"No," said Arnold. "You can't come on my side of the room." So Arnold packed by himself while Webster watched.

As soon as Arnold was out the front door, Webster ran back to their room—to Arnold's side. He tried out everything.

At dinner Webster sat in Arnold's chair. His piece of apple pie was bigger than anyone else's.

That night Webster, Old Bunny, and Pandy Bear climbed up
to Arnold's top bunk to sleep.

On Monday Webster's mother painted the kitchen Orange Sherbet. Webster painted the inside lower half of the pantry door Jonquil Yellow Glossy—all by himself! Webster thought Jonquil Yellow Glossy was the most beautiful color he'd ever seen.

His mother and father said he was a fine painter. And no one told him that he should have painted it better or different—or not at all.

On Tuesday Webster's mother baked a cake to celebrate how beautiful the kitchen looked. Webster helped. He did all the important things. He cracked the eggs and beat the batter. And he didn't have to fight over who got to lick the frosting bowl. It was all his.

Webster's friend Sam came over to visit on Wednesday. Sam didn't like wrestling or playing monster wars, so they drew monster pictures. Webster thought Sam was nice, but no one ever had to tell him to use his quiet voice. He was always quiet.

Thursday was rainy. Webster's mother said he could have a picnic lunch in his room. The soft fall of the rain outside was the only sound Webster heard as he fed Old Bunny and Pandy Bear their lunch.

Webster remembered the last picnic lunch in his room. He and Arnold had made a tent out of quilts and pretended they were camping out at night. They had to yell a lot to scare away some bears.

On Friday night before bed Webster's father read *Goodnight, Little Mouse* to him.

Webster liked it better when his father read *The Mousey Boys' Adventures* to him and Arnold. After the light went out, they would pretend they were the Mousey Boys and make up new adventures.

In the middle of the night Webster woke up. Something was strange and scary. He sat up and listened.

"I hear too much quiet!" he yelled, but no one heard him. It took Webster a long time to get back to sleep.

On Saturday morning Webster had to clean the whole bedroom all by himself. When he tried to make up the top bunk, the quilt fell down over the side of the bed and he couldn't pull it up.

Webster climbed down to try to figure out how to get the quilt up again. But then he had an idea. He took his own quilt and pushed it under Arnold's mattress. Then Webster climbed into the bottom bunk.

"Wait 'til Arnold sees my cave!" he said.

Webster had just brought Old Bunny, Pandy Bear, and some of his games into the cave when he heard the bedroom door open.

"What's this?" gasped a voice that Webster knew well. Arnold was home. Webster stuck his head out of the cave and thumped his chest.

"This is my cave and I am the caveman!" he roared. Arnold came closer to look.

"Say, that's not a bad cave," he said. "Can I come in?"

"I'll think about it," said Webster, but he pulled back a corner of the quilt, and Arnold climbed in.

Arnold sat in a corner of the cave.

"Grandma makes good cookies," he said, "but it's too quiet at her house."

"Well," said Webster, "it's not too quiet here!" And he whomped Arnold on the head with a pillow. Arnold jumped on him with a whoop, and together they rolled out of the cave onto the floor. Then Arnold hopped on his skateboard and went zooming around the room.

"Giddap, dinosaur!" he yelled. "The caveman is after us!"

Webster hurried to the top bunk.

"Here comes the caveman!" he yelled just before he jumped down on Arnold.

Much later in the middle of the night Webster woke up.
From above he heard Arnold's soft snore. He smiled.